CLASSIC TALES
ONCE UPON A TIME
GOLDILOCKS
AF372571

ONCE UPON A TIME, THERE WAS A FAMILY OF BEARS THAT LIVED IN A HOUSE IN THE FOREST.

EVERY DAY, MAMA BEAR WOULD PREPARE PORRIDGE FOR BREAKFAST AND PLACE IT IN THREE BOWLS.

THE LITTLE SON AND PAPA BEAR ALWAYS
WOKE UP TO THAT DELIGHTFUL AROMA THAT
FILLED THE HOUSE.

MAMA BEAR WAS VERY HAPPY BECAUSE
SHE PREPARED THE PORRIDGE WITH ALL HER
LOVE FOR HER FAMILY.

ON A SUNNY AND WARM DAY, THE BEARS DECIDED TO TAKE A WALK IN THE FOREST WHILE THE PORRIDGE COOLED DOWN.

BUT, WITHOUT REALIZING IT, THEY LEFT THE DOOR OPEN WHEN THEY WENT OUT.

WHILE THEY WERE OUT, GOLDILOCKS, A VERY
CURIOUS LITTLE GIRL, APPEARED. SHE LEFT
WITHOUT TELLING HER PARENTS AND WENT
FOR A WALK IN THE FOREST.

WHEN SHE APPROACHED THE BEARS' HOME, GOLDILOCKS SMELLED A DELICIOUS AROMA OF PORRIDGE.

AS THE DOOR WAS OPEN, GOLDILOCKS ENTERED WITHOUT ASKING FOR PERMISSION. UPON REACHING THE KITCHEN, SHE SAW THREE BOWLS OF PORRIDGE ON THE TABLE. SHE WAS HUNGRY AND COULDN'T RESIST: SHE TOOK A SPOONFUL FROM EACH, BUT FOUND THE PORRIDGE IN THE SMALLEST BOWL THE MOST DELICIOUS AND DEVOURED IT ALL!

THEN THE LITTLE GIRL WANTED TO REST.
WHEN SHE ENTERED THE LIVING ROOM, SHE
SAW THREE CHAIRS AND TRIED THEM ALL.
HOWEVER, AS TWO OF THE CHAIRS WERE
TOO BIG, SHE SAT IN THE SMALLEST ONE.
SUDDENLY, THE LITTLE CHAIR BROKE, AND
SHE TOOK A BIG TUMBLE!

WITH HER LITTLE BELLY FULL, GOLDILOCKS FELT SLEEPY AND WENT TO LOOK FOR A PLACE TO REST. SO, SHE CLIMBED THE STAIRS AND SAW THREE BEDS. SHE LAY DOWN ON ALL OF THEM BUT LIKED THE SMALL BED THE MOST, WHICH WAS WARM AND SOFT.

WHILE THE GIRL WAS SLEEPING, THE BEAR FAMILY RETURNED FROM THE FOREST READY TO EAT THE PORRIDGE. HOWEVER, WHEN THEY ENTERED THE KITCHEN, THEY SAW THE TABLE ALL MESSED UP AND ONE OF THE BOWLS EMPTY. THEY GOT VERY ANGRY!

SO, THE BEARS WENT TO THE BEDROOM AND FOUND GOLDILOCKS SLEEPING. UPON SEEING THAT STRANGER IN HIS BED, THE LITTLE ONE STARTED TO CRY.

GOLDILOCKS WOKE UP TO THE NOISE AND WAS STARTLED TO SEE THE BEAR FAMILY IN FRONT OF HER.

GOLDILOCKS GOT SO SCARED THAT SHE JUMPED OUT OF BED AND RAN THROUGH THE FOREST TOWARDS HER OWN HOUSE.

AFTER THAT DAY, SHE LEARNED THAT SHE SHOULD NEVER GO OUT WITHOUT TELLING HER PARENTS AND THAT SHE CANNOT ENTER ANYONE'S HOUSE WITHOUT PERMISSION.

THE END